Hello, Reader!

They are two best friends
and they LOVE their tutus.
They wear their tutus everywhere—
even to the beach!

You will like this funny story
about tutus, dancing, and friendship!

For Barbara, of course,
with a hug for Emilie.
— S.B.

Library of Congress Cataloging-in-Publication Data

Brownrigg. Sheri.
    All tutus should be pink / by Sheri Brownrigg; illustrated by Meredith Johnson.
        p.   cm.—(Hello reader)
    "Cartwheel books."
    "Level 2."
    Summary: Two little girls attend ballet class and eat strawberry ice cream afterwards.
    ISBN 0-590-90737-9
    [1. Ballet dancing — Fiction. 2. Friendship—Fiction.] I. Johnson, Meredith, ill. II. Title. III. Series.
PZ7.B8243A1 1992
[E]—dc20   90-40325
                                     CIP
                                      AC

32 31 30   11 12 13 14/0

Printed in the U.S.A.
First Scholastic printing, April 1992

40

ALL TUTUS
Should Be

Pink

by Sheri Brownrigg
Illustrated by Meredith Johnson

Scholastic Inc. Cartwheel B·O·O·K·S ™

New York Toronto London Auckland Sydney

I love my new tutu!

It's pink.

I had another pink tutu,
but it got too small for me.

My dog Pepe-Pierre
wears it now.

Emily has a pink tutu, too.

She's the best friend
I ever had.

We wear our tutus everywhere.

To the grocery store.

To the movies.

Even to the beach.

The real reason
we have our tutus
is dance class.

Our favorite person is
our dance teacher,
Ms. Yvonne.

She used to be a famous
pink tutu dancer.

We know this because
there are pictures of her
at the studio.

We want to grow up to be
famous pink tutu dancers, too.

But I think we
would wear our tutus
even if we were
truck drivers!

Dance class looks like fun,
but it is hard.

Sometimes it's so hard,
Emily thinks she might faint.
And we want to quit.

Then we look at ourselves in the mirror and see how great we look.

And we keep on dancing.

Tutus make a magic *swoosh* sound
every time we move.

Sometimes we move a little extra
to make extra *swooshes*.

Others in class
wear their tutus
only on stage.

For Emily and me,
all the world is a stage.

After dance class
we are so famished!

We need to eat ice cream.
Strawberry only, please!

If we drop some on our tutus, it doesn't matter.

They're pink, too.

That's why
all tutus should be pink.
I love my new tutu!